ANNONCIADE

\+ + + + + +

Elizabeth Spires

PENGUIN BOOKS

PENGUIN BOOKS
Published by the Penguin Group
Viking Penguin, a division of Penguin Books USA Inc.,
40 West 23rd Street, New York, New York 10010, U.S.A.
Penguin Books Ltd, 27 Wrights Lane,
London W8 5TZ, England
Penguin Books Australia Ltd, Ringwood,
Victoria, Australia
Penguin Books Canada Ltd, 2801 John Street,
Markham, Ontario, Canada L3R 1B4
Penguin Books (N.Z.) Ltd, 182–190 Wairau Road,
Auckland 10, New Zealand

Penguin Books Ltd, Registered Offices:
Harmondsworth, Middlesex, England

First published in the United States of America by Viking Penguin,
a division of Penguin Books USA Inc. 1989
Published in Penguin Books 1989

1 3 5 7 9 10 8 6 4 2

LIBRARY OF CONGRESS CATALOGING IN PUBLICATION DATA
Spires, Elizabeth.
Annonciade/Elizabeth Spires.
p. cm.
ISBN 0 14 058.638 5
I. Title.
[PS3569.P554A83 1989b]
811'.54—dc19 82-2901

Printed in the United States of America
Set in Garamond No. 3
Designed by Ann Gold

THE PENGUIN POETS

ANNONCIADE

Elizabeth Spires's poems have appeared in *The New Yorker, The New Republic, Grand Street, The Paris Review, Antaeus,* and other publications. She lives in Baltimore with her husband, Madison Smartt Bell, and teaches at Goucher College and the Writing Seminars at Johns Hopkins. In 1986–87 she was the Amy Lowell Travelling Poetry Scholar.

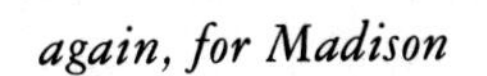

again, for Madison

Contents

Acknowledgments

Some of the poems in this book first appeared in the following magazines:

American Poetry Review: "Josephine"; "Primos"
Boulevard: "Thanksgiving Night: St. Michael's"; "Thaw"
The Georgia Review: "The Woman on the Dump"
Grand Street: "The Bells"; "The Comb and the Mirror"
The Iowa Review: "Sunday Afternoon at Fulham Palace"
The New Criterion: "The Beds"; "Victoriana: Gold Mourning Pendant with an Eye Painted on Ivory"; "Rosa Tacchini"; "Annonciade"; "February Origami"; "0°"; "The Celestial"
The North American Review: "Mutoscope"
The Ohio Journal: "Falling Away"
The Paris Review: "/ /"
Partisan Review: "Stonington Self-Portrait"
Poetry: "Fabergé's Egg"; "Profil Perdu"; "Black Fairy Tale"
Vassar Quarterly: "The Little Boys"; "Glass-Bottom Boat"; "Patchy Fog"
The Yale Review: "The Needle"

The author would like to thank Tracy Brown, William Gifford, and Robert Richman for their unfailing support and encouragement during the writing of this book.

Many of these poems were written with the assistance of an Amy Lowell Travelling Poetry Scholarship, which the author gratefully acknowledges.

"0°" also appeared in the anthology *The Direction of Poetry* (Houghton Mifflin, 1988).

I

+ + + + + +

The Beds

LONDON

Each day, I take the lift from the sublet down to the ground floor.
Out on the street, I pass the shop that sells the beds,
the sumptuous beds, made up each morning anew, afresh,
by smiling clerks who please their own moods,
doing the beds up one day in flaming sunrise and sunset tones,
and the next, in shades of white on white, with satin piping,
pillowcases expertly threaded with ribbons and bows,
like a bride's too-delicate underclothes.
And yet, nobody sleeps in the beds, makes love in the beds.
They wait, like a young girl with too much imagination,
to be taken away for a weekend in the country,
to a great house where lovers flirt and scheme
in preliminary maneuvering, but know, in the end,
what beds are for. Know, no matter what they do,
all will be plumped and tucked and smoothed,
all made as it was, by knowing maids the morning after.

The anxious clerks stare out at the soiled street,
the racing cars and taxis, the passersby, waiting for money
to stop, walk in the door, and ask to buy a bed.
There are circles under their eyes,
as if they've been sleeping badly.
Beds must make way for other beds,
pillows for other pillows, new sheets, new lives!
The seconds tick on the big clock
a block from the bed shop, the minute hand moves
with a jerk, and suddenly whole hours have flown,
        the day vanishes,
pulled by an unseen hand through a small hole in the sky
somewhere in the darkening East End.

Night falls so quickly on this street of Dream Merchandise!
Now all of us reverse ourselves and change direction
to come home to well-intentioned stews with husbands and wives,
yesterday's leftovers made to stretch so economically,
my heels on the sidewalk clicking in silver tones
like the small change in my pocket falling end over end over end,
all that remains of a day's hard buying.
Already the new moon is backlighting the city's towers and spires,
illuminating shadowy shop windows up and down Fulham Road.
It drapes itself casually across the beds,
like the misplaced towel or bathrobe
of a woman who has just stepped out for the evening,
wearing new evening clothes, made up so carefully
she can't be recognized, who secretly knows
she will not be coming back until morning
to sleep, if she sleeps then,
in the perfect bed of her own making.

The Little Boys

The little boys are lined up, two by two,
in short gray pants, white shirts, blue cardigans.
The bow-tied schoolmaster stops them at the corner
by resting his heavy hand on the head

of the first boy. The light is against them.
A snaking line of twenty twitching minds
jostles and shoves as it comes to an unwilling
standstill. The term has just begun, each fall

a new beginning for everyone except the unsmiling
schoolmaster. October always rushes by, he thinks,
but this year his boys have dwindled down
a little even as they've grown, inch by awkward

inch, into a little manhood. Already the first form
divides and subdivides along Darwinian lines
into bullies and crybabies trying not to cry, trying
and failing to hold back the hot smart tears

that doom them to years of crybaby torture.
Bad dreams, bad words, bad smells, and small moments
of heroism: that's a little boy's life.
The line shuffles and shifts, the stoic schoolmaster

secretly wishing the light would give them
the go-ahead. Green to red now, like the season
turning, cars slide to a stop as the no-nonsense
schoolmaster firmly raises his hand, as if to push

a heavy door open, and marches his boys up the street
into a manly future. Fearful or brave, all must follow,
all must do as he says or suffer the consequences.
Chins up, heads high, zippers unzipped, and shoelaces

dragging, they disappear, the quicker
duplicitous ones already plotting an overthrow
where no mercy will be shown, no prisoners taken.
There is no turning back for a little boy.

Fabergé's Egg

SWITZERLAND, 1920

Dear Friend, "Called away" from my country,
I square the egg and put it in a letter
that all may read, gilding each word a little
so that touched, it yields to a secret
stirring, a small gold bird on a spring
suddenly appearing to sing a small song
of regret, elation, that overspills all private
bounds, although you ask, as I do, what now
do we sing to, sing for? Before the Great War,
I made a diamond-studded coach three inches high
with rock crystal windows and platinum wheels
to ceremoniously convey a speechless egg to Court.
All for a bored Czarina! My version of history
fantastic and revolutionary as I reduced the scale
to the hand-held dimensions of a fairy tale,
hiding tiny Imperial portraits and cameos
in eggs of pearl and bone. Little bonbons, caskets!
The old riddle of the chicken and the egg
is answered thus: in the Belle Epoque
of the imagination, the egg came first, containing,
as it does, both history and uncertainty, my excesses
inducing unrest among those too hungry to see
the bitter joke of an egg one cannot eat.
Oblique oddity, an egg is the most beautiful of all
beautiful forms, a box without corners
in which anything can be contained, anything
except Time, that old jeweler who laughed
when he set me ticking. Here, among the clocks
and watches of a country precisely ordered
and dying, I am not sorry, I do not apologize.

Three times I kiss you in memory
of that first Easter, that first white rising,
and send this message as if it could save you:
Even the present is dead. We must live now
in the future. Yours, Fabergé.

Josephine

Josephine has been in the zoo since 1953.
Her mate, Horatio, died in 1985 . . .
—Placard at the London Zoo

In the big birdhouse, questions and answers,
wolf whistles, love songs, and desperate calls for help
are batted back and forth like tennis balls.
Hellohellohello, cries the mynah to no one in particular,
a white woodpecker tapping, obsessively tapping,
an arrhythmical line below the screeks and wails
of black bulbuls, saffron toucanets, and lilac-breasted rollers
in the cages next to Josephine's, a great Indian hornbill.

Josephine is stylishly got up, in black and white
tail and breast feathers. A horny yellow plate
flattens the top of her head like a pillbox hat;
her big beaked bill curves comically downward, like a banana.
The walls and ceiling of her cage are painted sky-blue,
except for a small brown dirty patch where Josephine,
in a fit of pique, furiously attacked the illusion.
Calmly now, she shifts from one foot to the other,
preening and posing, the effect slightly Egyptian:
Josephine as the Sphinx. Josephine with her back turned.
Josephine in noble profile, showing off her bill.

Her keepers exist because she exists.
Quietly they pass, in green uniforms,
each with a pale green grape for Josephine.

Once it was Josephine and Horatio. Horatio and Josephine.
Never one without the other, reliable as old bridge partners.
Now it is Josephine alone in a big world
where four-footed creatures would, in an instant,

make a quick snack, an *hors-d'oeuvre,* of Josephine.
She prefers not to think about it.

A hammer striking an anvil. A microphone being tuned.
The racket in the birdhouse is intense and loud.
Josephine makes no sound. I look her straight in the eye.
Her pupils dilate and contract, cagily taking me in
as I take her in, an old cross-eyed dowager.
She yawns. Blinks.
Another keeper, another grape, will appear eventually,
relieving the stunned tedium of the moment.
Josephine will wait for that to happen.

Victoriana: Gold Mourning Pendant with an Eye Painted on Ivory

Who made this thing?
An eye staring
without blinking,
laid down on the dead

white of ivory by paint
and brush, pearls ringing
the pendant's oval as if
grief could be transformed

into a cold and costly
object. How calmly the eye
contemplates the scenes
put before it: my birth,

a tear in time's fabric
I crawled through quickly,
headfirst, quickly forgetting
the blood, the pain, the lights.

Halfway into my journey,
the cold wind of coincidence
throwing my shadow against yours
to meet and marry for life.

And the deaths in a line
on the horizon, black
silhouettes waving to us,
though we don't wave back.

An eye that sees too much
and yet sees nothing.
Why do I hate it so,
hate the artist who

would work the body into
a relic of hair and ivory,
who, in love's memory,
would pluck the eye

from the socket,
leaving the living
model blind in one eye?
I will turn from the art

of eyepainting, so distant
from hands, lips, heart.
Until we die, we live
in an everlasting present

of physicality that feels
things blindly, inch by inch,
by sense, by sound, by fingertips.
Let the dead learn from us.

Sunday Afternoon at Fulham Palace

PUTNEY BRIDGE, LONDON

A Sunday afternoon in late September, one of the last
good weekends before the long dark, old couples
taking the air along the Thames, sunning themselves,
their arms and legs so pale, *exposed,*
eyes closed against the slanting autumn light,
while the young press forward, carry us
along in the crowd to the fair at Fulham Palace
where a few people have already spread blankets and tablecloths
for the picnics they've brought, laughing and talking
as they wait for the music to begin at three o'clock.
Inside the palace gates, a man inflates
a room-size, brightly painted rubber castle,
the children impatiently waiting for walls and turrets to go up,
the spongy floor they like to jump on.
The palace is empty. The Bishop gone.
Now overfed goldfish swim slowly round and round
in the crumbling courtyard fountain, and farther on,
a white peacock stands still as a statue,
still as a stone, whether in pride or sorrow
at being the last of its kind here I don't know.
A low door opens into the Bishop's walled garden, but once
inside nothing miraculous or forbidden tempts us,
just a few flowers and herbs among weeds
(unlike those illuminated scenes in books of hours),
the past passing away too quickly to catch or recognize.

Out on the other side, we pick our way
among booths put up for the day,
one woman, predictably, passing out pamphlets
on nuclear winter and cruise missiles, as if she could stop it alone.

The Fulham Band takes its place on the platform,
the conductor announcing as the overture
"Those Magnificent Men in Their Flying Machines,"
the crossed shadow of coincidence, of airplanes from Gatwick
passing over at two-minute intervals, touching us
for a moment before they fly into the day's
unplanned pattern of connections, the music
attracting more of a crowd, men, women, and children
making their entrances like extras in a movie,
in pairs, in families, no one alone that I can see
except one girl, no more than ten,
lagging behind the others, lost completely
in a vivid, invisible daydream until her mother finds her,
brings her back with a touch on the arm,
and the daughter says, unbelievably,
"I was thinking about what kind of anesthesia
they'll give me when I have my first baby."

The future expands, then contracts, like an eye's iris opening
and closing,
walling me into a room where light and sound come and go,
first near, then far, as if I had vertigo.
It is easy, too easy, to imagine the world ending
on a day like today, the sun shining and the band playing,
the players dreamily moving now into Ellington's "Mood Indigo."
Easy to see the great gray plane hovering briefly overhead,
the gray metal belly opening and the bomb dropping,
a flash, a light "like a thousand suns,"
and then the long winter.
The white peacock. Erased. The goldfish in the fountain

swimming crazily as the water boils up around them, evaporates.
The children's castle. Gone. The children. The mothers
        and the fathers.
As if a hand had suddenly erased a huge blackboard.
Thank God you don't know what I'm thinking.
You press my hand as if to ask, "Am I here with you?
Do you want to go?" pulling me back to this moment,
to this music we are just coming to know, the crowd around us
growing denser, just wanting to live their lives,
each person a *nerve,* thinking and feeling
too much as sensation pours over them
in a ceaseless flow, the music, as we move to go,
jumping far back in time, the conductor oddly choosing
something devotional, a coronet solo
composed, and probably played here, by Purcell
        three centuries ago.
All is as it was as we make our way back along the Thames
to Putney Bridge, the old souls still sleeping unaware,
hands lightly touching, as the river bends in a gentle arc
around them. Mood indigo. The white peacock.
The walled garden and the low door.
As if, if it did happen, we could bow our heads
and ask, once more, to enter that innocent first world.

The Bells

Here goes, my brave boys.
—Inscription on a bell,
Northenden, Lancashire

Whether it be true or not,
the bells will have their say,
ringing the common and uncommon
anniversaries on Sundays and wedding days,
tolling funerary sermons, the faithful
bellringers dressed in the cassocks
of plainness, their featherweight souls
lifted easily skyward, then lowered
gently, until the soles of their feet
again touch solid ground and they wait,
good children, for the change summoning
them back to heaven. Through upraised arms,
through coarsely braided bellropes,
desire or willed intention flows,
electric, and grace comes trickling down
upon whoever rings, new ringers ringing
with the old in chains of never-ending
sound from Cornwall to Northumberland.

So, too, with us.
We live for the sounding, often pulled
speechlessly upward, then hurriedly let down,
as this evening I am pulled by evensong
down Bury Walk to St. Luke's on Sydney Street
where paths twist and curve around
the multitudes of bright burning flowers,
tulips set like the bells, mouths upward;
obeisant, flame-red, perilously they bow
and lean a little out of themselves,
as I do, toward a ring of shadows

in the tower's high cloud-ridden windows,
the ringers beginning the evening's
business with a round, pure sound
flying in four directions over Londontown,
bright arrows that pierce all who listen
until, like martyrs, we all fall down,
struck by the doubles and triples
of existence. What moments are these,
tongued wholly with inexpressibles?
What ghosts descending? How shall we
put them to use, with what abandon?
The signs are there if we would listen, see.

Mutoscope

Swirl and smash of waves against the legs
and crossgirders of the pier, I have come to Brighton,
come as the fathers of our fathers came,
to see the past's Peep Show.
On two good legs, on one, they came,
veterans and stay-at-homes of the Great War,
all casualties, to stroll the West Pier's promenade,
past bands, flags, and minstrel shows,
past Gladys Pawsey in a high-necked bathing costume
riding her bicycle off the high board,
past Hokey-Pokey and Electric Shocker,
to the old Penny Palace, pennies burning hotly
in their hands, the worn watery profile
of Queen Victoria looking away from it all.
I bend to the mutoscope's lit window
to see "What the Butler Saw": a woman artlessly
taking off her clothes in a jerky striptease
I can slow down or speed up
by turning the handle of the mutoscope.
Easily I raise her from darkness—
the eye eternally aroused by what it can't touch—
to watch her brief repeating performance
that counts for so little. Or so much.
I can't be sure which.
Abruptly, *THE END* shuts down the image, but her story
continues as she reverses time's tawdry sequence
to dress and quickly disappear
down a maze of narrow streets and alleys
filled with the ghostly bodies and bodiless ghosts
of causality, the unredeemed and never-to-be-born

bearing her along to a flight
of shabby stairs, a rented room where she is free
as anyone to dream her dreams and smoke a cigarette,
smoke from the lit tip spiraling
in patternless patterns toward the room's bare light bulb,
the light I see her by harsh, violently
unforgiving, as she makes tomorrow into a question
of either/or: to leave this room, this vacancy
forever, or go on exactly as she has before.
Old ghost, your history is nameless and sexual,
you are your own enigma, victim
or heroine of an act of repetition that, once chosen,
will choose you for a lifetime.
I peer into the tunneled past,
so small, so faraway and fragmentary,
and yet, not unconnected to what I am now.
Dilapidation upon dilapidation, Brighton
is crumbling, fading to sepia tones,
as your unfunny burlesque continues past
your life, perhaps past mine,
the past preserved and persevering,
the sentimental past.

Rosa Tacchini

11-22-1872

Hides, horns, hooves, tallow, wool:
the commerce of the world drives men, takes lives.
Homeward bound, from Buenos Aires to Italy,
the ocean our glittering toy, we were dragged
from St. Mary's Roadstead by a gale, just off
the Scilly Isles, success turning on our lips
as good wine turns to bad in the unreasoning bottle.
Paper was our downfall, we struck the Paper Ledge,
I at the bow, the blind eyes in my head
responsible. Washed up near Carn Near,
I lay with the years, my beauty going
quickly, as yours will, weather coarsening
my fine features into wind-roughened wood.
Come closer. Read me with fingers.
Learn by looking in my eyes how elements
conspire to drag the living down to never-to-be-
fathomed depths and give new life to the dead.
I am fixed on a thin horizon, my punishment
to see now what I didn't see then. Forever will I live
on this windswept tropical isle, buoys ringing
in my head, signaling rocks and shallows
I must watch out for. I am still changing!
Who speaks to you from dark depths?
Whose voice enchants and holds you, as innocent
beauty can't, in a briny net woven out of hardship?
It is I, the daughter of time.

Primos

OFF LAND'S END

As an unlucky match is singled out and struck
against a matchbox, we struck the Seven Stones
on the 24th of June, in the Year of Our Lord, 1871,
and quickly foundered, the crew of eleven drowned,
except for you, Vincenzo Defilice, the odd man
who left all behind to swim away and toward
nothing, no one, hope your only handhold
against the sliding, slippery waves of a chance throw.
An unreal parade of cargo floated past,
laughably useless, a chair and writing table,
corked bottles of spirits, a bobbing pair of boots
a ghost might use to lightly walk across the water.
Why, why were you not yet drowned, too?
Numbly, you sifted the acts of a lifetime,
the pettiness and petty generosities, anger, greed,
and self-defeating loves, searching for a sign or clue
your life was worse or better than the next man's.
And then a miracle began to happen: a human form,
no mermaid, appearing beside you in the waves,
wearing a gilded crown, her face uplifted
to the clouds, serene as a saint's. Wake up, Vincenzo!
Again I am pulled backward through time's current
to buoy your artless, dreaming heart.
Face to face, we lock in an embrace more urgent
and prolonged than any two landlocked lovers
ever exchanged, riding the swells for hours,
then parting, exhausted, your reasons expedient:
you swam toward land or land's illusion,
a rich man in possession of a story more fabulous
than the disenchanted fictions of any shipwrecked novelist.

Years pass as quickly as the turning of pages.
Now in the underwater dark of taverns and bars,
you cross yourself and tell your tale of water
to surefooted unbelievers hungry to hear
a drunken sailor's story of wholly improbable rescue.
The world is full of grace and second chances
for a few. You were a saved man.
I speculate upon your future.

The Comb and the Mirror

based on the Cornish folktale of
the mermaid of Zennor

Two-natured, loving my world
but loving you as much,
I came every seventh day
to lonely Zennor parish
and hid outside the church.
From fish to forkéd human,
changing my form I came,
to hear you, Mathey Trewhella,
nakedly sing your hymns;
I drowned in the songs you sang.
Week after week I returned,
until Highsummer Sunday
you spied my lovesick face
in the church's great glass window,
a stranger among the saints.
On new unsteady legs
I tried to run away,
not wanting you to net me,
but you followed anyway,
or would in vain have followed.
Held back by humankind
(they warned you of my charms),
you thought but didn't say,
Love cannot help itself.
O bitterly they tell,
bitter to lose one of theirs,
how moonlit nights you searched,
moonstruck and bewitched,
the caves of Pendour Cove
for my flashing mermaid's mirror.

Waist-deep you waded in,
down Neptune's Steps you walked,
and only thought one thought,
Love cannot help itself.
As I myself found out.
Night after night, they tell
how I wrap you in my hair
and we drown in love's delight,
how you like to comb my hair
with a comb of tortoise shell.
Or so the fishwives swear.
But I revise their tale.
Down Neptune's Steps you walked,
backward I swam and you followed,
no spell used I, no words,
to take you to deep depths
where self gives back the self
in love's unreflecting mirror.
Netted unlike to like,
we spent one night together
before a chill dawn broke
and washed away the dream.
I woke in waves and found
my arms around you, drowned.
Never now on earth,
I swear a lover's oath,
shall pairs of lovers find
such harmony of mind
as we for one night shared;

by my heartless comb and mirror,
I will that man and wife
—jealous, mortal, proud—
shall see love turn to spite,
their first love not survive
the weather of their lives.

Profil Perdu

In 1949, in Menton, after long lovemaking
one afternoon, they drew each other:

each kneeling, in turn, by the bed
as the other slept or drifted,

the pen tracing on paper what
the body knew, the strangely lovely

angle of her face thrown back on a hill
of white pillows, and he, in his turn,

wanting if he wants anything never
to leave this room. Each has fallen

softly back into the body as one
might fall into a dream of high blue

meadows in midsummer, midsummer time
leaving them another hour, two,

before they must make their way,
shivering, down the dew-stained mountain.

O let us gently close the door
on love's impromptu sketch and leave

them as we would be left, here
among the long shadows of a room

we have entered without reflection,
all grief or grievance put aside

to draw the body's burning
outline on white sheets, white paper.

Their life, and ours, the evidence.

Annonciade

But should the fiery essence of the soul think on its high origin, and cast aside the numbing stain of life: then will it carry with it, too, the flesh in which it lodged and bear it also back among the stars.
—Prudentius, Fourth Century A.D.

It is not right for me to look upon the dead,
And stain my eyesight with the mists of dying men.
—Euripides

Morning, and the sounds of the valley float
slowly, like smoke, up the tiered mountain
to our windows. A cock's crow, too early,
sets off a chain of barking dogs and donkeys,
the screams of a peacock, all reassuring
that the world below is awake and waits
to take us back when we are well enough to go.
Here at La Maison de Repos, each day
has the same beginning: alone, the eye opens,
sentient, to a room unchanged by any dream
or nightmare, relieved or disappointed
to be transported back to the waking dream.
An arm throws open a shutter, flooding
the doubting mind with the brilliant
light of the Midi that changes white
shadowed sheets on the crumpled bed
into a still life of desire and absence.
Mountains and blue air and the sea,
faraway waves soundlessly pounding the lit shore,
the horizon blurred, the azure coast,
wash upon wash, bleeding like a watercolor:
these things I see as I steady myself
at the window, still wanting to be alive.

Soon eye and body join in a rhythm
of small tasks a child could do

—though no child lives here—
a shaky hand dressing itself, carefully
buttoning buttons and putting on shoes,
before it joins the slow parade to breakfast.
I am among the fortunate who shuffle
and shift for themselves; others
are wheeled, or walk on crutches, or are led.
It is at breakfast that the curtained ambulance
sometimes slips away, delivering one
from our midst to health or oblivion.
A place at the table is empty, a face
gone forever, but nothing is said
to note the absence of the missing one.
Our silent circle contracts, or grows
larger to accommodate a new arrival
who pauses, uncertain, in the door,
unsure of what will happen next, waiting
to be politely questioned or ignored.

All morning we are touched by the shadow
of the Annonciade on the hill above,
the monastery bells ringing prime, calling
a scattered few to prayers and morning mass,
good nuns and brothers ascending,
in ones and twos, the 500 worn stone steps
of the Chemin de Rosaire, one old soul
all in black holding her rosary
as she climbs, counting the beads and steps
that take her, one by one, to heaven.
It would be good to be like her,

to simply *believe,* to question nothing,
her life an unwavering road she blindly
knows. Soon others follow, the fallen-away
and sightseers on holiday, grateful
after the long climb to enter the cool cavern
of the church, crossing themselves
or genuflecting out of almost-forgotten habit,
lighting a votive candle for five francs.
Time's silence surrounds them, held
in the steady flame of the Sacred Heart,
in the armored effigy of a nameless crusader
who lies on a low altar in the crypt,
hands clasped in an attitude of prayer,
as if at any moment the warrior
soul will wake, leap up, and lead
the sleeping body to Apocalypse.
Most visitors cannot stay very long;
they speak in guilty whispers
and move through the church like intruders,
move quickly past the apocryphal
remains of martyrs, splintered fragments
of bone and strands of human hair
in shining jewel-encrusted caskets,
the stoppered crystal vials of blood
and tears, relics handed down for centuries
by the silent monks who lived here once,
who watched the crippled pilgrims come,
kneel down, and pray for a guardian spirit's
intercession, then sometimes rise
and throw away their crutches, favored

by a miracle. The old order's gone,
only a few lay caretakers left
to take care of the grounds and sell
postcards of the view to tourists.

It is *we,* the ill and ill-disposed,
who now live closest to annunciation,
who watch the darkness closing in
each end-of-the-world night,
who need the mountain air for health,
the silence for our shattered nerves,
the isolation to contain contagion.
We are our missing useless parts:
a chest coughs into a cup and cannot
stop itself; two bandaged eyes
wait for the touch of a surgeon
who anoints or takes away clear sight;
the body helplessly submits to the probe,
to the omniscient X-ray eye that searches
for the small dark spot on the lung,
the glowing bone that will not mend.
Others wait for the pill, the injection,
the cup that will not pass,
wanting and yet not wanting to know
if dark malignancy remains,
if health, that faraway kingdom,
will be given back to them.
How can such suffering be chance?
Surely the spirit chooses its affliction
and makes it manifest, watching itself

fall and retreat from the world to atone,
as holy hermits did, for some secret
failing only its own heart knows.

It is easy by afternoon to become
delirious, to believe, as one lies
insubstantial in the shuttered room,
that the omnipresent flies traveling
mad circuits are sent from heaven
to reassure us that heaven, too, is imperfect.
We are close to heaven here, so high
above the world. Are we the chosen?
Chosen for what? Will our suffering
redeem others? Or only ourselves?
Surely in time we will each be blessed
with annunciation: I will rise
from this pallet of rest and recrimination
and step nakedly back into the world,
pulled down the mountain's winding road
to the lit auberge where the concierge
will calmly greet me, asking no questions,
knowing my journey was difficult.
He will bathe my forehead with a cool cloth,
wiping away pain and the memory
of pain, until my clouded mind
is a clean slate, my headache gone.
Then will I take my place among the guests
who drink the good wine and eat
the steaming food, who raise their glasses
in a toast to *health,* to *earth,*

to my return. Quietly will I sit there,
like a ghost, as the last light
of the setting sun slips through me
before it, too, is lost behind the mountain.
The air will deepen into shades of blue
and darker blue, a cock will crow,
betraying its desire for dawn,
and the bells of the Annonciade
will gravely ring compline.
Then all will fall silent.
Once more I will briefly belong
to the world before I lay me down
on the white pillowcases of the Elect,
the lights of stars and houses coming on,
shining unrepentant, as if Earth
and Heaven had joined in a solitary moment
of love, the deceived and deceiving
eye, as it falls to sleep, feeling
strange intimations of happiness.

Menton, France

II

+ + + + + +

Falling Away

Memory: I am sitting at my desk in sixth grade at St. Joseph's Elementary in Circleville, Ohio. It is a winter morning in 1964, and we are in the middle of catechism. The classroom is old-fashioned, with high ceilings and wood floors, the crucifix above the front blackboard in a face-off with the big round clock on the back wall. The room smells of chalk and soap and dust. There are six or seven tall windows which can be opened in the spring and fall but which are shut tightly now. The heating pipes knock. The room is uncomfortably warm, a little steamy. The early morning snowfall has put all of us in a dreamy, slow-motion mood, everyone, that is, except for our teacher, a study in black and white, dressed in a heavy black habit and black veil, white wimple, collar, and bib. A crucifix hangs from a black rope belt knotted around her waist; she has told us that if she holds it and sincerely repents her sins at the moment of death, her soul will fly straight to heaven.

Sister M—— points outside with her long wooden pointer, the same pointer that often comes down with a *crack!* on the desks of unsuspecting daydreamers, bringing them back to this world with a start. Outside, each snowflake is lost in the indistinguishable downward spiral of the heavy snowfall. The voice that is not a voice comes back, her voice, imagined, reconstructed from memory: *How many souls are in hell? More than all the snowflakes that are falling today, yesterday, tomorrow.* I try to imagine a number that large, an infinite number, and cannot. Then I try to follow the path of one individual snowflake in its slow, yet inevitable, drifting descent, but lose it in the swirling pattern of white against white.

The lesson continues: *How long will those lost souls pay for their sins? For all eternity.* Eternity. How can we, at eleven years old, she must be thinking, possibly be able to conceive of just how long eternity is? *Imagine the largest mountain in the world, made of solid rock. Once every hundred years, a bird flies past, the tip of its wing brushing lightly against the mountaintop. Eternity is as long as it would take for the bird's wing to wear the mountain down to nothing.*

Ever after, I connect hell and eternity not with fire and flames, but with something cold and unchanging, a snowy tundra overshadowed by a huge granite mountain that casts a pall over the landscape. Like the North or South Pole in midsummer, the sun would circle overhead in a crazy loop, day passing into day without intervening night, each object nakedly illuminated, etched sharply in light and shadow, unable to retreat into night's invisibility. If I were unlucky, I'd be there one day, for *forever,* dressed in my white communion dress, white anklets, and black patent leather shoes. And there would be others, too, a field of stopped souls who couldn't move or speak, but who suffered the cold, suffered inaction, without sleep or forgetfulness. Like children playing freeze tag on a playground, the field of souls would stretch over the horizon past the vanishing point. The only moving thing a small black spot in the sky, the bird that flew high over our heads once every hundred years when the century flipped over, like the odometer on a speeding car.

Clock-time and eternity. Darkness and light. A poem lies in the experience of that grimly metaphysical catechism class, one that I can't write, though I've tried many times. It comes to me in shards and fragments, frozen, like I am, when I enter the memory:

. . . and so I imagined the edge of the world,
a great domed space, black stones
and ice, where I'd stand forever
not dressed for the weather,
my heart beating fast as a metronome.
And the bird flying past
would come so close, I'd hear
its heart beat fast as my own.

If the bird needed food,
what did it do?
Did it sing as it flew,
a shining black syllable?

Now when I look in your eyes—
two tunnels running backward
to infinite light, infinite darkness—
I think what Time will do to those
who admit so freely what they have to lose.
White dress, black shoes,
what is a life anyhow?

Titled "A Lesson in Eternity," the poem remains unfinished, unresolved, the final question unanswered. I had a dream recently, a more benign version of a recurring nightmare. Usually, I am back in grade school or high school completing a requirement that I somehow missed or deliberately avoided. I am in my adult mind and body among children, carrying the burden of adult memory and consciousness. I am threatened with not passing, not graduating, and thus, not going on to the next "step," if I don't make up for childhood omissions. It is a dream that suggests, in its many different variations, that I have not finished "old business." In this dream, however, I am back at St. Joseph's not as a student but as a teacher. Teacher of what? I haven't been told. No one is there. I walk through the empty classrooms, a dream landscape of small wooden desks in neat rows, polished and shining, and freshly washed blackboards, all of it held in suspension, waiting for something to happen. A bell to ring. The classrooms to be flooded with shouts and light. It doesn't matter that the school has been closed for years. Standing in the dark hallway, I'm thinking how I'll finally see through the keyhole into that polarized world of good and evil, guilt and absolution, that even a fallen-away Catholic can't escape. After all, I have all time. Have all eternity.

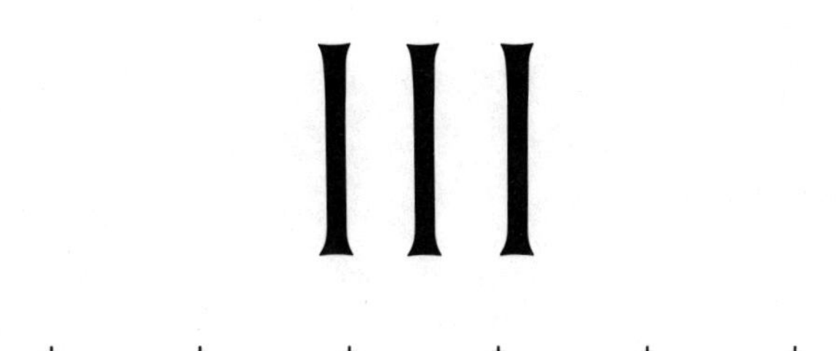

Thanksgiving Night: St. Michael's

CHESAPEAKE BAY

A scarred night, fog, the sky a streaky white,
as we walk out, out on a finger of land
that points like a sign to World's End,
and step from land to water, the pier creaking
under us like the springs of an old bed.
We scare, by being here, a heron
from its hiding place; it changes itself
into blue smoke and wind and flies west
over the world's bright edge, leaving behind
an old ghost under the pier, the stiff ribs
of a skiff buried in black water. Eaten
by air, by water, each year there is less to it.
Behind us, a world too-human waits,
a crisscross of familiar streets and houses
painted with fresh paint, and lit storefronts,
their goods arranged in careful tiers and rows,
offering us the new, the young, the bright.
Skeletal night! Soon the tide will run out,
stranding the skiff, like a great beached fish,
in shallows, each bony rib countable, monstrous,
a feast of past, present, and future holidays
mingling, like wine in water, until all are one,
the dead, living, and not-yet-born gathered
around the great table to suck the sweet
marrow from the kill, as if there will always
be, for us, a tomorrow tomorrow.

Glass-Bottom Boat

KEY WEST

In the Cubano diner, tiny cups
of black, black coffee, hot and sweet,
and chipped blue china plates
of black beans and yellowtail,
fished by the fishermen
as the sun came up this morning.

Yesterday out on the reef,
we looked through the floor of the boat,
through layers of clear, clean water—
windows looking into other windows—
down to the floor of the world,
shallow, pliant, and shifting.
There, schools of yellowtail
swam through the living coral,
bright as stained glass,
cast into underwater constellations
both strange and familiar:
a flower, a brain, a cathedral.
Suddenly a shadow parted the school—
as if a cloud had just blotted the sun—
a barracuda swerving as they swerved,
and nothing they could do.
After it fed, the two halves joined,
the missing ones unmourned,
all as it was before.

If I could live for a thousand years,
ten thousand, would ever I see
the great family of men, women, and children,

both preying and preyed-upon,
swimming as freely as the yellowtail?
Would that be heaven or hell?
Each naked human face a candle
joining other candles in a procession
spanning many centuries, entering
the cathedral of live stone
whose heavy doors are cast
with scenes from our own lives,
moving as moving pictures move,
until the reel runs out.
In that world-without-end hour,
will the future read us in relief,
blindly touching each raised
and burnished scene with fingertips,
the ejaculate word forming on their lips,
an *O!* and then again an *O!*
of terror and astonishment?
O how will they sing knowing what they know?
Streaming through time, they see
our approach, we are plotted
in space, our light outlives our lives
and sends a signal far into
the future: *the past is alive!*
Dead and dark for a long time,
we are as stars to them,
stars wishing to be wished on.

Black Fairy Tale

Who were you that day you left your parents
standing on the platform, waving black handkerchiefs
—How young they were then!—
and you waving back, you with money in your pocket
        and your grin,
as the train began to move, first slowly, then slowly
speeding up, the whitewashed houses of that village
falling flatly back into the past
as you sped forward into a morning stilled by fog,
by enchantment, dreaming of a woman
bending over you, pouring milk into a glass,
whispering, *Drink this, Drink this.*

So many years have passed!
You wake to the noon sun burning a hard, black outline
around the fallow fields, the shimmering trees and houses,
shadows doubled into themselves, hiding,
the train speeding faster, ever faster,
birds on the wires, black birds,
marking off milestones, chuckling to themselves.
Smiles, gestures, currency, the few words
your parents taught you, like *love, farewell,* and *courage,*
are useless now, you're crossing unfamiliar borders
quickly, much too quickly, your death and birth connected,
as the crow flies, by a straight line on a map
although you never wanted, did you, a journey as simple as that?

For one ten thousandth of a second
you stall at midpoint, caught between twin cities,
twin infinities, just long enough to glimpse

a pale child beckoning from the black edge of the forest.
Return, you must return, by following the black fairy tale,
the one your parents kept from you,
locked in the black book at the back of the closet.
Bits of bread, fluttering rags snagged on hedges,
will show you the way if you look, if you look.
Who must you save? Shadows are showing themselves,
touching this thing and that with their shadowy spells,
a fat red sun is disappearing as you enter
the clearing where the empty cottage stands,
its door swinging on hinges that sing, *What use, What use.*
Nobody's there, nobody that is
except a crow, hunched in a tree,
its feathers coal-black and shining, eyeballing you,
each eye as empty as the barrel of a gun,
making a *click, click, click,*
now that you've arrived.

The Red Boomerang

for Adrian, 9

Do you remember? February
and the blue sky lay in a flat curve
above the curving earth we stood on,
the same sky I spent my childhood under,
yours now, both hand-me-down and new,
the small white houses of the small Ohio town
ringing the empty park, their windows
pairs of eyes, set low to the ground,
staring at an empty baseball diamond,
three sets of swings, a merry-go-round
and slide, the park's far side bounded
by train tracks running rapidly away
in opposite directions, two quicksilver lines
meeting at a mystic vanishing point
too far for us to ever walk to.

I hadn't seen you for half a year.
Heart-high, you were growing up quickly;
by summer you wouldn't be a little boy.
All was unfair fractions and parallels,
two wishes, two parents wanting you
to choose, choose only one of them, not two.
But how could a nine-year-old decide,
when nine wasn't an even number to divide?
Tightly, you held the untried boomerang,
bent like an arm at the elbow,
alive, a thin wish ready to fly
into a cold sky of possibility.

Up, up it went, not like a bird
but like a blurred red word silently
shouting, *goodbye, goodbye.* Halfway
to somewhere, it paused, changing
its mind, and flew back again, falling
out of reach as you ran to meet it.
Patiently you practiced your throw
as, minute by minute, time stole
the afternoon, our seven-league
shadows almost tall enough to touch
the untouchable horizon. Again you threw,
your small force greater than my own.
Again the boomerang turned, parabola
of the heart's desire, in a faithful arc
toward its only point of origin: you.
Caught in a one-handed catch!
And you were smiling.

February Origami

A room, empty and cold.
A daytime moon, cheek
scraped off, hanging by a thread,
looking in at what you do.
You sit on the floor cross-legged,
folding and refolding
a square of paper, a letter,
white writing like swirling snow
on a scroll. As a child,
didn't you sit by the window
coaxing raucous paper cranes—
red, green, and yellow—
to fly into a sky of blue?
Now what could you say or do
to make a piece of paper fly away?
You watch your hands, two
birds, shape paper into
a white diminishing thing.
Here is my heart, you write,
quill sipping ink from a bowl.
Here is my heart.
Take it if you have to.
Two wings beat in your hands.
The injured moon, sheer
as rice paper, slips away.
It is a white, white day.

0°

These nights when the wind blows,
I lay my head on the pillow,
I lay my head on white feathers,
white down, tag ends of Memory.
White feathers, white down,
I'm wrapped in a nightgown stiffening,
year by year, against the cold.
My arms hug the pillow, light
as a feather when we lie in love's
weather, but tonight I sleep alone,
the closet full of skeletons that grin
in the chilly breeze. Starving,
they climb love's zero by degrees,
as I will, the pillow dreaming
furious dreams. Dreams not my own.

Puella Aeterna

I was a changeling in a changeling world
of appearance I walked through slow or fast,
feeling tensions and warps in the fixity
of chairs and tables, the gravity of stones:
all things that are, so simply, themselves.
As we are not. The smallest object
might be distorted as time's bright flow
poured suddenly into my room from a door
in another part of the house opening
or closing (the way my face this morning,
after a night of sleeping badly, looked
out unhappily from a breakfast spoon,
reminded it had changed, was changing).
I felt the animate presence of things
alive, auras and flickerings surrounding
each breathing object, just as the pose
of saints in stained-glass windows, banded
by haloes and black outlines, is heightened,
intensified, by the rising sun shining through
the stopped tableau of their ordinary lives.

Each night in astral dreams, I flew above
the peaked and pointed spires and steeples
of the whitewashed town, the streets like spokes
on a wheel, converging at the circle's center,
flew over the enthroned moon, fat and full
as a pumpkin, trying in vain to touch
its shifting, shimmering surface that rippled
and flowed like the nightshirts of sleepers
caught in the crosswinds of a dream. Below,

the townspeople pointed speechlessly upward
at a girl flying with outstretched arms
away from everything she knew. Believe
or disbelieve a story different from your own.
I was a chameleon, a dissembler, a conjuror
of form. Unbounded by gravity, I had
no motive except to *live,* no destination,
had yet to learn that love is a power
releasing darker powers that would
change me, sweep me away forever.

The Diviner

As lightning passes from cloud to branching tree,
forked and stripped like a body, love struck me
where I stood and I was changed, changed into wood.
Lost in that first falling, I grew toward arms
that never would hold me: a girl, a sapling.
Spring was my brief unfolding.
By summer, heat scorched the ground around me.
Autumn stripped me of pride.
Winter clothed me in cruel clothes, the spirit
stiff and unmoving, moved only by merciless wind
until it took the inhuman shape of love denied.
Midwinter, the sun a pale disc in the sky,
hope was reduced to a simple will to survive,
birds circling me with their starving cries,
pecking the bare ground, small scavengers of nothing.
I held my crooked arms aloft, a scarecrow
wanting to scare nothing, and raved at my diminution.
I had lost everything! And still I was spellbound.

For seven years I stayed, stayed where I stood,
became the creature of my own becoming
before the spell was lifted and I was free,
free never to love you again. On hands and knees,
I drank in long drafts from the river of forgetting,
a woman's curious face staring into mine.
Then did I weep bitterly for years lost, stirring
the water to dissolve that face, so much like mine.
In my hand, a willow wand I'd use to divine direction.
A journeyman now, I left that ravaged landscape
no point on the compass would ever find,

in fine leather boots, my hair cut short like a man's.
As men did plunder, so would I, trading illusion
for illusion, singing oblivion's old song,
A heart for a heart, an eye for an eye . . .

The Needle

Eye to eye, I
thread love's needle and see
a narrow slice of room which I,
too large, cannot pass into
until my task is done.
Your favorite shirt is torn.
Worn for too many years,
the threads above the heart
have pulled apart, a ragged tear
I'll mend and mend
again, helpless against the words
we sharpen to a fine point
against each other. My needle
catches the light, flashes and bends,
joining the soft cloth as a surgeon might
stitch the chest, tenderly
closing the wounded heartflesh.

Mended, the tear is gone,
the shirt shows nothing.
So that now when I put down needle
and thread and climb the twisting stairs
to our narrow bed, I'll pass
easily through the needle's eye
to follow sleep's narrative, a white thread
sewn into the blurred blue horizon,
every trace of memory and premonition
erased, your face on the pillow
blank and nameless as the moon.

//

Two verticals lie down,
each to the other, a horizon,
each to the other,
alone and unaligned.
But can we not bend Time
until we touch and cross
unafraid to overrun
the map that Nature put us on?
My altered angle runs away
from yours until, halfway
around the world, we meet again,
the map's four corners gone,
our parallels concluding
at the fevered poles where
day for one is never-ending
night for its opposite.
It's there that barefoot angels
dance to music that we cannot
hear, but try to, being human.
We are two lines, pulled
up & down the globe by Time
& Choice & Circumstance
until Eternity marries us,
& two become one.

The Walk

Past the skittish sheep in the sheeplot,
past the pond dried up by the drought,
to the woods with the windfall trees,
with long strides you covered the distance,
one for each two of mine.
Behind us the fence that marked boundaries,
strands of barbed wire at the top;
ahead the high hill of your childhood
the first snow would soon cover up.
Thistle and burdock and loosestrife
clung to the legs of our pants,
worked their way through the fabric
and stung the living flesh.
You knelt by a bush of red berries named,
you said, Hearts-Bursting-With-Love,
and handed me one, blood-red like emotion,
and kept just one for yourself.
Then we came to a scattering of feathers
and a shiver went down my spine,
a cardinal's crimson feathers a warning
to anyone who walked this pathless path
that the heart could be torn out
by talons and hauled into the sky.
I would have turned back then.
But you kept on.

High on the rushing hill, a prospect
of years before us, you spun me
in four directions until I was a compass
of feelings, the needle swinging wildly.

Smoke curled from the chimney
        of a little white house in the valley
where a man and a woman had married,
        married and had a child. Unseen,
we watched them working, raking dull leaves
        into piles. Tomorrow or the next day,
they'd set a match to it all.
        But clouds were gathering abruptly,
and thunder rumbled nearby;
        a drop fell on my cheek,
then another, as if I were crying.
        Shaking her fist at the clouds,
the woman ran into the house,
        the screen door slamming behind her,
while the man stood still in the yard,
        hands raised to the opening sky.
Love was around them there, if love
        is a falling off, first anger,
then surrender, loss piling onto loss.
        What could protect us now
from November's bone-chilling downpour,
        from the signs of our own diminishment
in the windfall trees, in the pond,
        in the scattering of red feathers
when the heart is descended on?
        Only the measure of a vow,
never to forsake each other,
        held between finger and thumb,
the hard four-chambered berry,
        Hearts-Bursting-With-Love.

The Woman on the Dump

Where was it one first heard of the truth? The the.
—Wallace Stevens

She sits on a smoldering couch
reading labels from old tin cans,
the ground ground down
to dirt, hard as poured cement.
A crowd of fat white gulls
take mincing, oblique steps
around the couch, searching for
an orange rind, a crab claw.
Clouds scud backward overhead,
drop quickly over the horizon,
as if weighted with lead sinkers.
The inside's outside here,
her "sitting room" *en plein air:*
a homey triad of chaise longue,
tilting table, and old floor lamp
from a torn-down whorehouse,
the shade a painted scene
of nymphs in a naked landscape.
The lamp is a beautiful thing,
even if she can't plug it in,
the bare-cheeked, breathless
nymphs part of the eternal
feminine as they rush away
from streaming trees and clouds
that can't be trusted not to change
from man to myth and back again.

The dump's too real. Or not
real enough. It is hot here.
Or cold. When the sun goes down,

she wraps herself in old newspaper,
the newsprint rubbing off,
so that she *is* the news as she
looks for clues and scraps
of things in the refuse. The *the*
is here somewhere, buried
under bulldozed piles of trash.
She picks up a pair of old cymbals
to announce the moon, the pure
symbol, just coming up over there.
Abandoned bathtubs, sinks, and stoves
glow white—abstract forms
in the moonlight—a high tide
of garbage spawns and grows,
throwing long lovely shadows
across unplumbed ravines and gullies.
She'll work through the night,
the woman on the dump,
sifting and sorting and putting
things right, saving everything
that can be saved, rejecting
nothing, piles of tires
in the background unexhaustedly
burning, burning, burning.

Patchy Fog

This morning the lilies on Ames Pond,
pink and yellow cow lilies, spoked lilystars,
lie open waiting for the sun, and trees,
or the ghosts of trees, a mild smoky gray-green,
hover and point toward the unseen, heaven
of unbelief, as fog boils and rolls
off the road in patches that come and go,
like the call and its echo of the Great Blue Heron
that lives alone in the pond's long shadow.

A floating world of doubt the heron
must step into, wading the pond's shallows,
back and forth, to feed on *tree, lily, sky,*
with hungering heron eye until the morning's
curtain parts and shafts of sunlight make
the heron cry, cry out, to see itself defined,
bright burning outline in sky's water, and beat
its wings and fly, smoke into smoke, toward heaven,
mind that masterminds the pond's closed circle.

Thaw

The living souls of trees
have gathered round this pool
to look at themselves in the water.
The surface shimmers and ripples,
the sky is upside down, look
and you'll see the clouds
drifting along the bottom.
White and unsullied and proud,
they are blown like sheets on a line;
the smallest of small winds,
and they shiver with anticipation.
Spiders and waterstriders flit,
in a trance, here and there.
Chit-chit, sings a brazen bird,
nameless, hidden somewhere.
Chit-chit, chit-chit, it repeats,
chiding a young girl's airs.

I'm no one, I'm nothing, I'm waiting—
all root, bark, branch, bare twig—
for love to appear and free me
after a winter of blind belief.
My naked arms reach upward
to nakedly touch the sun;
the elements can change me,
change wood into flesh and blood.
Anyone watching right now
would be surprised to see
a woman step out of herself,
her hair, her hands in leaf.

Stonington Self-Portrait

Old sinner, pilgrim of doubt,
today I had a vision of you, myself
in thirty years, sitting
in a rusted, wrought-iron chair
bolted to the selfsame stony hill
I've stared at days now. The hill,
matted with grass, wildflowers,
only a stone's throw
from my bedroom window, the sea's door.
Gulls toss above it, like blown bits
of paper, the tide recedes,
and still no new moon rises.
An isolate figure, you pull
your sweater closer, tighter,
accusing the past, accusing the future
that insists, year by slow year,
"Love loves itself! Loves nothing else!"
But you can't go back on our pact,
the body's bargain with itself.
Now nothing can save you
unless I do, the past rushing in
to fill the future's narrows.
Thirty years. You've paid the price.
Or I will. Because today
I saw something remarkable:
a cloud in the shape of a woman,
a woman in the shape of a cloud,
form coupling with fluid
loveliness, moving and restless.
Soon you'll be myth, a cloud

floating in a sea of blue,
artfully drifting nowhere
I can imagine, what's known, what's earthly,
of no importance whatsoever
in the life that follows this one.

Stonington, Maine

The Celestial

Korean Buddhists traditionally keep this breed in temple ponds.

When God made the angels, a man made me,
turning my gaze heavenward for a purpose
I know and do not know. The world
is a sphere that mirrors my pond, all things
have order here: the sun rushes
across the sky, pulling the moon
on a pale fishing line, and I see myself
printed among the stars, a great fish
swimming in the night's black sea.
Weeks pass into months, the year going
from warm to cool, bright to dull,
ginkgo leaves drifting down,
down, to slowly settle on pondbottom,
like pieces of ragged gold foil. I, too,
am streaked with gold along my spine and tail
but am valued for my eyes, bulging
blue-green globes larger than my soul,
a small clear bubble wrapped around the purity
of nothing. It slips with each breath
from my astonished mouth and flies rapidly upward
—as prayers will sometimes—
but always catches on the pond's rough skin.
I twin until there are many of me.
I begin and begin.

O Ghosts of the Upper World,
don't we see you in your shimmering robes,
peering through seven watery veils
that, lifted, reveal nothing behind the curtain?
Don't we hear you chanting?

Bells call you to the temple and you hurry away,
orange robes streaming, as if
you were running headlong into a violent wind.
We do not hurry as we take the world in
through our mouths, as sensation
passes through us, unconcerned
to be swimming toward where we've already been.
To be, not do: that is the lesson
we try to teach you.
We have heard of an underworld where fire
is the transforming element and water burns
quickly away to vapor,
but will not see it ever.

Our gaze is upward and forever.

FOR THE BEST IN PAPERBACKS, LOOK FOR THE 

In every corner of the world, on every subject under the sun, Penguin represents quality and variety—the very best in publishing today.

For complete information about books available from Penguin—including Pelicans, Puffins, Peregrines, and Penguin Classics—and how to order them, write to us at the appropriate address below. Please note that for copyright reasons the selection of books varies from country to country.

In the United Kingdom: For a complete list of books available from Penguin in the U.K., please write to *Dept E.P., Penguin Books Ltd, Harmondsworth, Middlesex, UB7 0DA.*

In the United States: For a complete list of books available from Penguin in the U.S., please write to *Dept BA, Penguin,* Box 999, Bergenfield, New Jersey 07621-0999.

In Canada: For a complete list of books available from Penguin in Canada, please write to *Penguin Books Canada Ltd, 2801 John Street, Markham, Ontario L3R 1B4.*

In Australia: For a complete list of books available from Penguin in Australia, please write to the *Marketing Department, Penguin Books Australia Ltd, P.O. Box 257, Ringwood, Victoria 3134.*

In New Zealand: For a complete list of books available from Penguin in New Zealand, please write to the *Marketing Department, Penguin Books (NZ) Ltd, Private Bag, Takapuna, Auckland 9.*

In India: For a complete list of books available from Penguin, please write to *Penguin Overseas Ltd, 706 Eros Apartments, 56 Nehru Place, New Delhi, 110019.*

In Holland: For a complete list of books available from Penguin in Holland, please write to *Penguin Books Nederland B.V., Postbus 195, NL–1380AD Weesp, Netherlands.*

In Germany: For a complete list of books available from Penguin, please write to *Penguin Books Ltd, Friedrichstrasse 10–12, D–6000 Frankfurt Main 1, Federal Republic of Germany.*

In Spain: For a complete list of books available from Penguin in Spain, please write to *Longman Penguin España, Calle San Nicolas 15, E–28013 Madrid, Spain.*

In Japan: For a complete list of books available from Penguin in Japan, please write to *Longman Penguin Japan Co Ltd, Yamaguchi Building, 2-12-9 Kanda Jimbocho, Chiyoda-Ku, Tokyo 101, Japan.*

FOR THE BEST POETRY, LOOK FOR THE 

☐ **TANGO**
Daniel Halpern

The poems in Daniel Halpern's sixth collection explore encounters with landscape, with friendship, with isolation, and with love and death.

"*Tango* has its own definite character and imprint—real, original, and strong." — Robert Penn Warren

88 pages *ISBN: 0-14-058588-5* **$10.95**

☐ **LAST WALTZ IN SANTIAGO**
And Other Poems of Exile and Disappearance
Ariel Dorfman

From the land of Pablo Neruda, here is a searing collection of poems about torture and resistance, horror and hope. In Ariel Dorfman's world, men and women choose between leaving their country or dying for it.

"Deeply moving . . . stark and at the same time oddly radiant"
— Margaret Atwood *78 pages* *ISBN: 0-14-058608-3* **$8.95**

☐ **CEMETERY NIGHTS**
Stephen Dobyns

In his sixth book of poems, Stephen Dobyns explores a full range of human experience—from fabulous storytelling to explosive passions of domestic life, from vital distortions of familiar myths to strange tableaux of creation and death.

"Dobyns has fashioned his remarkable poems into a real book, not simply a collection." — *The New York Times Book Review*

100 pages *ISBN: 0-14-058584-2* **$9.95**

☐ **AGAINST ROMANCE**
Michael Blumenthal

A new collection from the winner of the Academy of American Poets Peter I.B. Lavan Younger Poets Award, *Against Romance* explores the possibilities for love in an unromantic time and an indifferent, beautiful universe.

"Advancing by leaps and loopholes of inference, Michael Blumenthal's poems . . . are never far from joy." — Anthony Hecht

108 pages *ISBN: 0-14-058600-8* **$8.95**